Powers of the Knife

BONTLE SENNE

cover2cover
books

Published in South Africa by
Cover2Cover Books

cover2cover.co.za

Copyright © Bontle Senne

First published 2016

ISBN: 978-0-9946744-5-6
e-ISBN: 978-1-928346-22-7

Typesetting and book design: Robin Yule
Cover design: Wiehan de Jager
Cover art: Kit Beukes
Illustrations: Pete Woodbridge, Studio Woo
Editing: Lisa Compton
Proofreading: Sean Fraser
Printed and bound by Shumani Mills

CHAPTER **1**

Nom has no choice but to fight. The
gang has her surrounded. She's all alone
behind the tuck shop. School ended
hours ago. The Trouble Gurlz gang are
always picking on Nom. They pinch
her when no one is looking or trip her
on her way home.

She pulls her fingers into a tight fist,
getting ready to throw a punch if she
has to. *These Trouble Gurlz are so stupid,*

Nom thinks.

But they are also pretty, and Nom does not think she is. Her lips are too fat and her nose is too big – but, like her dad says, looks aren't everything. Nom is smart and she can fight. Nom thinks that's much better than running around after stupid boys. She raises her fists to her chin.

One girl leans forward and flicks Nom on the ear. Nom tries to swat her hand away, but she's too slow.

"Not so tough with no teachers here to see, are you, *Nomthi*?" says a girl with long braids down her back.

"My name is Nom," she says, swallowing down any chance that she will cry in front of them.

All the girls look at each other and laugh.

"Your name is Nomthandazo. You

can't be cool just by pretending to have a cool name," says a girl wearing school shoes but no socks.

"*Wa bora*, Nomthandazo. You're boring and you're ugly," says the one with the braids. One of the other girls spits into the dirt. Another girl giggles.

That's it, thinks Nom. In a flash she throws her fist into the ear of the girl with the braided hair. Nom punches her so hard that her hand hurts. The girl bends over, swearing and crying. Her friends all start shouting now. They are really mad.

"You should not have done that, Nomthandazo," says Precious, the prettiest of the Trouble Gurlz. "Now we have to teach you a lesson."

Nom takes a few steps back, but the girls are coming closer and closer. Her back is about to touch the wall and she'll have nowhere left to run. One of the shorter girls pushes her left shoulder with both her hands. Nom loses her balance. She falls flat on her bum in the red dirt.

"Precious!" shouts a voice from in front of the tuck shop. "Is that you?"

The Trouble Gurlz halt in their tracks and look at each other.

"Is that you, Zithembe?" Precious calls back to the voice.

Zithembe appears behind the tuck shop, facing the group of girls. "It's me," he says with a small smile. "What's going on here?"

"This rich girl thinks she can say what she wants and do what she wants in this place. *We* run this school. *We* say what's what," says Precious, folding her arms.

Zithembe nods his head to show

that he understands what they are saying. "I see," he says. "But you know who her dad is, right?"

All the Trouble Gurlz look at Precious. Of course they know who Nom's dad is. Everyone knows Jabu. He's the big boss of the taxis in this township, part of the North Star Taxi Association. No one messes with Jabu.

Precious nods but doesn't say anything.

Zithembe asks, "You know I live there, right? My aunt works in their house. We live in the back room."

"Ja, so?" Precious says. "What do I care?"

"Come on, Gurlz! Do me a favour. Bra Jabu is going to give me a hot *klap* if he finds out I saw his daughter getting beat up and I didn't do anything about it."

Most of the girls now have their arms folded and are looking from Precious back to Zithembe, trying to decide what to do.

"And, *yho*," Zithembe continues, "he would not be too happy with you either …"

He gives them a minute to think about that. None of them really knows what Bra Jabu would or would not do. But they have heard enough stories around the township to know you don't take chances with guys like him.

"Precious, I'm begging you. *Mngani wami*, my friend, just let this girl go," Zithembe says.

Precious is silent for a moment. "OK," she says finally, "but she better watch her mouth. Next time maybe I won't be so nice."

Zithembe shrugs and fakes a smile.

He notices that the other girls don't look happy that he's stopped the fight. *These Trouble Gurlz are crazy*, he thinks. They are always fighting and getting into trouble.

Zithembe offers a hand to Nom, who is still sitting on the ground. He is trying to help her get up, but Nom hits his hand out of her way. She stands up by herself and dusts off the back of her school skirt. With one hand she scoops up her school bag, but her eyes stay on the other girls.

Zithembe tilts his head to the side to show Nom that they need to leave. They walk away, with Nom in front. As soon as they get to the other side of the tuck shop, they hear the Trouble Gurlz talking.

"We can't just let her go like that," one girl says.

"People will think we are getting soft and start taking advantage," another one adds.

Zithembe speeds up and takes the lead. He pulls Nom by the arm to make her get out of there faster.

"I don't care that her dad is Bra Jabu. *We* rule this school. We need to show her who makes the rules," says a third one.

Precious must have agreed with them because Zithembe sees two of the girls running towards them. Each of them has a big, sharp rock in one hand.

"Run!" shouts Zithembe.

Nom and Zithembe run all the way
home. Nom lives with her dad and her
mom, Ma Phumi. At Nom's house there
are always people coming and going.
North Star taxi drivers, their friends,
and Jabu's friends, cousins and aunts
have all come to stay with them for at
least a few days. There are never really
any other kids around, though – except
for Zithembe.

When Zithembe and Nom reach the gate of the house, one of the drivers pulls it open and closes it behind them. As soon as they are safe, Nom falls onto the small patch of grass and laughs.

"I can't believe we just did that!" she says, shaking her head and still laughing.

Zithembe is surprised by Nom's reaction. Those girls could have really hurt her and here she is, laughing about it. Zithembe knows he doesn't have much money but at least he has sense. He knows when to fight and when to run. Zithembe doesn't say anything to Nom. He puts his hands in his pockets and turns around to go to his room.

"Wait!" Nom says, standing up. "Why did you help me?"

The truth is, the only reason he

helped Nom is because he respects her father. He has lived with his aunt, Zinhle, in the back rooms of Nom's house for almost two years now, and they haven't had much to do with each other. Aunt Zinhle isn't too bad, but he misses his grandmother. The schools are better in the city, though, and that's why she sent him away to live with his aunt, for a better life.

"I don't know," Zithembe answers finally.

"Well, I owe you. I was going to fight them, but there were too many of those stupid Trouble Gurlz. I'm sure my dad will give you are least R100 when he finds out that you helped me."

Zithembe's eyes go big. "I don't want your money!" he says.

"Wait, I didn't mean it like that ..." Nom begins to explain, but Zithembe is walking away.

"Hey!" Nom calls after him. He ignores her.

Nom runs up behind Zithembe and pulls his shoulder so that he has to turn around.

"Hey, I'm sorry, OK? I didn't mean to make you mad," she says.

"But I *am* mad," Zithembe says.

Nom looks down at the ground and says quietly, "Look, I don't have a lot of people who would help me like that. I don't really have friends. I don't know how to thank you. I'm sorry, OK?"

Nom doesn't say it but Zithembe knows she doesn't have friends because she's a 'rich girl'. People are jealous. It's not her fault.

"OK," he says. They stand there for a few seconds. Neither of them knows what to say.

Then Nom asks "Can I show you something?"

"What?" he asks.

"Just let me show you. It's something I've never showed anyone. It's my secret. I want to prove that I'm really sorry, Zithembe," she explains.

Zithembe kicks at the grass with one foot. He's never been inside the big house where Nom lives. Sometimes he helps with cleaning or fixing the taxis in the yard. Bra Jabu gives him some money to cut the grass too. But he's never been inside the house before.

Zithembe tries to act cool and quickly puts his hands in his pockets. He doesn't want Nom to know that his palms are sweating. "OK" is all he says.

Nom leads the way into the house. As they pass through the kitchen, Zithembe is relieved that Aunt Zinhle isn't there to ask any questions. They hurry to Nom's room, and once they are inside she shuts the door behind them.

Nom's room is as small as Zithembe's, which surprises him but somehow makes him feel better. She's cut out pictures from magazines and stuck them all over her walls. Nom goes to a small desk by the window and pulls open the bottom drawer. She takes out a shiny blue box with a picture of a bird flying on the top of it. Zithembe is busy looking at the movie posters on the wall when Nom puts a knife right in front of his face.

"What the —?" Zithembe says, raising both hands to cover his face and stepping back quickly towards the door. Nom obviously pulled the knife out of the box but now she's pointing it at him. In the light from the window the handle of the knife shines a bright blue colour.

Nom quickly says, "It's what I wanted to show you. It's my knife."

"Your knife?" Zithembe asks. *This girl is crazy*, he thinks.

Nom nods her head and says proudly, "It was a gift from my aunt who died before I was born. My dad gave it to me but told me never to use it to hurt anyone. This knife is for helping people and protecting myself. He even showed me how to use it."

Nom smiles so that all her teeth show. When Zithembe doesn't say anything, she holds out the knife to him. "Here," she says. "Feel how light it is. The Trouble Gurlz would never mess with me if they knew I had this."

Zithembe doesn't want to tell her

that he thinks those girls have knives of their own. Instead he accepts the knife from Nom. The knife feels like it is gently shaking in his hand. He knows that it can't be moving by itself, but as he grips the handle tighter, the knife still feels like it is vibrating.

As Zithembe hands it back, he wants to say something about what he felt, but he doesn't. He tells himself that he must have just imagined it.

Nom puts the knife back in its box on the desk and turns around to face Zithembe.

"I know that other girls like things that are more normal, but this knife is … special to me. I have never told anyone about it. Not even my mom knows I have it," she says.

Zithembe is about to agree with her that the knife is cool. But before he can speak he notices it floating up out of its box. He points at it and says, "Nom! The knife … it moved by itself!"

Nom turns around to look and sees the knife. It hovers just above its box, floating in the air as though there is a hand they cannot see holding it up.

Before either of them can say anything more, the knife suddenly drops back into its box with a dull thud.

"Did you just see that? That's never happened before!" says Nom.

Just then, there is a scream so loud that it rips through the house. Someone is in serious trouble.

CHAPTER 3

Nom and Zithembe look at each other.
The scream comes again, this time even
louder. Nom is the first to run for the
door. Zithembe follows close behind.
They race out of the house and towards
the screaming. It is coming from where
the taxis are parked. When Nom comes
to a sudden stop, Zithembe crashes into
her. She loses her balance and almost
falls forward, but she recovers just in

time to stay on her feet.

Some of the taxi drivers have gathered around one of the drivers, who is lying on the ground. Zithembe remembers the driver's name: Mabegzo. Mabegzo is the one who is screaming. Tears are rolling down his cheeks and he is gripping his left foot in both hands as if he is afraid that it will fall off.

"It hurts! It hurts!" Mabegzo shouts.

"What happened?" asks Nom.

One of the other drivers, the fat one named Solly, turns to answer her. "Mabegzo says he stepped on something that cut through his shoe. But we can't see any glass or anything around, so we don't know ..."

"We have to take off his shoe," Zithembe says. All the men turn to look at him. None of them looks happy that he spoke without an adult asking him a question, but Nom backs him up.

"He's right. We have to take off his shoe to see what happened," she says.

While the drivers mumble something between them, one of them bends down to try to remove Mabegzo's shoe. Mabegzo flaps his arms at the driver wildly, like a bird trapped in the house. "Don't touch me!" he shouts.

The other drivers look at each other. "Come on, Mabs! We have to see so we can help you, *mfethu*," one of them says.

Again the driver bends down to try to remove his shoe again, but this time Mabegzo hits him in the nose and pulls him to the ground.

Three of the drivers move quickly to hold Mabegzo down while a fourth driver grabs hold of his shoe. Mabegzo kicks out his legs, shouting and swearing at his friends. He won't lie still for even a second. It takes all the men's strength to keep him from hurting anyone else.

Finally, they manage to get his shoe off. Nom leans in closer for a better look, but Zithembe keeps his distance.

He knows that this man Mabegzo has more anger and strength than even the noisy, drunk men walking home from the taverns early in the morning. Mabegzo looks like he would kill anyone who gets too close. From what Nom can see, there's a lot of blood but only a small hole in his shoe.

Then, just as quickly as he started fighting, Mabegzo stops squirming and shouting. His body goes completely limp. No one needs to hold him down any longer, but the men do not let go in case he is pretending. Mabegzo looks peaceful now, as if he has just fallen asleep in the yard with one shoe on and one bloodied foot.

The drivers all stand up and discuss quietly what they should do. While they are distracted, Nom creeps even further forward. Zithembe is ready to pull her back to the house when Mabegzo's eyes snap open. He twists his head quickly to look at Nom and then Zithembe.

He is smiling now, but there is no joy or happiness in his eyes. Mabegzo looks angry, but that's not all. The white part of his eyes has turned a bright, unnatural yellow. And Zithembe is not sure why, but he is convinced that Mabegzo looks *hungry*.

Nom jumps back and covers her mouth to stop herself from screaming just as Mabegzo hisses, "Stay away from the shadows. We're coming for you, little children."

Only Zithembe and Nom seem
to hear him say this. His words send
shivers from their heads to their toes.
Mabegzo keeps smiling as the yellow of
his eyes slowly turns to bright green.

CHAPTER 4

Nom lies on her bed, staring at the ceiling. She blinks away her tears to stop them from running down her cheeks and into her ears.

Nom can't remember ever being so scared that she cried. Sometimes she stayed up later than she was allowed and watched a scary movie on TV. After the movie, she would jump at every small sound in the house, afraid of who, or what, it could be. On those nights, she'd had to pull the blankets right over her head and wait under the covers until morning. But this was no movie. The monster she had seen was real.

The other drivers took Mabegzo to the clinic to have his foot looked at by a doctor. Zithembe had pulled Nom back into the house before she could do or say anything about what they had both just seen.

"Was that real?" asks Zithembe, sitting on Nom's bedroom floor with his back to the wall.

Nom sighs, pushing the air out of her mouth loudly. "I really don't know, Zee," she says.

Zee? Only Zithembe's boys, his best friends, call him Zee. Nom sees the confused look on his face and corrects herself. "Sorry, I meant Zithembe."

"No, it's OK," Zithembe says. "You can call me Zee."

Nom flashes him a quick smile, but it disappears as soon as she remembers those glowing green eyes. She sits up, bends her knees and hugs her legs close to her body.

"I still can't believe that Mabegzo turned into a monster," Nom says.

"When I was little, Mama used to tell me stories about monsters," Zithembe says, looking up at the ceiling.

"What were the stories?" Nom asks. She's still scared, but she is curious and can't keep the excitement out of her voice.

Zithembe turns to Nom and shakes his head. "They were just stories, Nom."

"I want to hear anyway. What did

she used to tell you?"

Zithembe takes a deep breath and says, "She said that monsters were not just imaginary things in bad dreams or movies. She said they were real. The monsters live in a dreamworld. It's like our world, but different."

"Isn't that just dreaming? Like when we go to sleep?" Nom asks.

"No, it's different. In a dream, you can fly or be late for school, but it didn't really happen. In a normal dream, you can die but you wake up afterwards. You're not really dead. But you can really die in the dreamworld. You don't wake up and you never get back to the real world. The monsters can hurt you for real."

"But if they're just in the dreamworld, everyone should be safe, right?"

Zithembe shakes his head. "Mama used to say that there is an army of monsters that have spent hundreds of years trying to break through into the real world. Every few years, one of them manages to do it and then starts doing terrible things to people."

"People like Mabegzo?" Nom asks.

"Anyone can be hurt. Monsters don't care how old you are or how good you are. They are just evil. They can all do different things. Mama used to say some of them can change their appearance so that they look like real people. Some can make you see things that aren't there."

"How did she know all of this?"

"She never told me," Zithembe says. "She told me that one day, when I was older, she would tell me everything. But 'one day' never came ..."

"Did she at least tell you how you stop the monsters?" Nom asks, frowning.

"She said children always had the best chance of fighting them. She told me that kids see things that grown-ups can't. We have the brains and the strength to get rid of all the monsters for good. All we need to do is find the magic," Zithembe says.

Nom has been listening closely and thinking about everything Zithembe is saying, but *magic?* She bursts into laughter. It feels so good to laugh that she can't stop. Zithembe folds his arms and looks at her.

When she finally stops laughing, Nom apologises. "I'm sorry, that was … I'm sorry. It's just – we're talking about monsters and magic like this is all real. Monsters are just made up to scare people. They don't really exist. And magic ... well, there's no such thing as magic."

"What about your knife?"

"What about it?" Nom asks.

"It moved by itself. It floated in the air and you saw it. How do you explain that without magic?" Zithembe asks.

Nom feels her face go hot. How *can* she explain that? Or what happened with Mabegzo? She saw the knife move with her own eyes. But how can Zithembe's mother's stories be true?

"Zee, what happened to your mom?" Nom asks, to change the subject.

Zithembe looks out of the window again and says slowly, "No one really knows. Mama just disappeared one day."

"Do you think she's dead?" Nom

asks in a quiet voice. She knows that this is not the kind of thing you should ask people about – especially if you are trying to be their friend. But the words just came out by themselves.

Zithembe doesn't say anything for a long time and Nom is sure she has hurt his feelings. She is about to apologise when he says, "No. I know everyone else thinks she is. But I still feel her with me. And if magic is real, I know I can use it to find her."

Nom does not know what to say to that. She just nods her head to show she understands.

"So, what now?" she asks.

"What do you mean?"

"We can't just leave things as they are and not do anything. We have to do something to help Mabegzo. We at least have to find out what's happening to him. I don't think the clinic can fix what he's got," Nom says.

"But what do you want to do? You don't believe in any of this stuff anyway, remember? What can we do?" Zithembe asks.

Nom thinks for a minute and then it hits her. "We have to get to the dreamworld," she says.

"What?"

Nom repeats, "We have to get to the dreamworld. You said that's where the monsters are. I think that's how we find out what magic we need to fix Mabegzo."

Zithembe gives her a look that tells her he doesn't understand why she's pretending to believe in all this.

"Look," Nom says, "I know what I said about monsters and magic not being real, but I can't explain the knife or what happened outside. I don't know … maybe your mom knew what she was talking about. We have to at least try to get to the dreamworld. And if we pull it off, it will make a great story."

Zithembe stands up and makes his way to Nom's door.

"Hey!" she says. "Where are you going?"

Zithembe says, "You said we have to get to the dreamworld. So let's go."

CHAPTER 5

Zithembe walks out of the room, not waiting for Nom to follow, but what choice does she have? She jumps off her bed and goes after him. Nom catches up with Zithembe just as he makes it to the gate.

Once they are standing outside on the street, he looks to the left and to the right. Nom turns to see his face scrunched up in concentration:

Zithembe is trying to decide which way to go. He turns right and Nom follows. The sun is lower in the sky. There are only a few hours left until it is dark.

They walk fast, not talking to each other. After ten minutes or so, Nom starts to see the places around them change. They walk deeper into the township to where people live in a mix of shacks and small new houses built by the government. Here there are no children playing on the street, just men sitting in little groups playing cards or dice on the side of the road.

Nom puts her hands in her pockets and tries not to look at anyone. Zithembe seems perfectly comfortable, but she has never been to this neighbourhood before.

When Zithembe finally comes to a stop, they are standing outside one of the older government houses. It looks like it was built in a hurry because it isn't totally finished. Half the roof is tiled and the other half is just a sheet of rusted metal. The metal looks like it could fly off the roof at any second and slice someone's head off.

The small sign on the door says 'Dr Naidoo's Africa Medicine Shop'. Nom pushes the door open and steps inside. She doesn't even knock, but it's too late for Zithembe to say something about that.

Stepping inside the shop is like walking into something you only see on TV. There are strange, smelly things all around. Jars of every size and shape, some open and some closed, are stacked on shelves.

Some jars contain brown powders, but there are just as many jars

containing pink, blue or green powders. Snakeskins, dried plants and belts made from animal hides hang from the ceiling. Ostrich and other bird heads sit in a pile on one of the low tables near a bag of shells.

"It looks like there's no one here. What is this place?" Nom says, her eyes wide as she tries to take in everything she sees.

"We're here to do some shopping," Zithembe says in a low voice. "We need supplies to get to the dreamworld."

"So, Zee Zee, what are we looking for?" Nom asks, wrapping her arms around herself in a tight hug.

He gives her a look to show her that 'Zee' may be OK but 'Zee Zee' definitely isn't. Nom laughs, but it's a nervous laugh, and she stops in case Zithembe can hear the fear in her voice.

He mustn't start thinking that she's a baby who can't handle this stuff.

She's scared because this place is dark and smells funny and has all kinds of dead things in it. *I'm scared*, she thinks, *but that doesn't mean I can't handle it.*

Zithembe says, "Mama said that you needed three special things to get to the dreamword."

"Things like what?" Nom asks, looking at the many animals tails nailed to one of the walls.

"The first one is your knife," he says.

"My knife?"

"It's a magical weapon. It must be. You saw how it floated up in the air by itself," Zithembe explains.

Nom remembers what they saw. She couldn't explain it then, so maybe her knife *is* magical.

Zithembe continues, "We're looking for the other two things we need to get into the dreamworld. We need branches from the *umphafa* tree. The branches have two rows of very sharp thorns. People believe that the thorns that point backwards tell you never to forget where you have been. The thorns that point forward tell you to always look ahead, to what is coming next."

"*Umphafa*? Why does that name sound familiar?" Nom rubs her arms from her shoulders to her elbows and back up to her shoulders, as if she is trying to warm herself.

Zithembe is looking at the jars on the shelf and does not seem to notice that Nom can't stand still. "Families use the branches to bring back the spirits of family or friends who have died far from home. The family goes to where the person died and they use the branch to carry the spirit of the dead home. Once they get home, they bury the branch but also the person."

Nom shivers. Her father had once gone to Pretoria with that kind of branch. He had to bring home his brother, Nom's uncle, who had died in a car accident. The branch was treated like it was her uncle. They even set it a place to eat at the table at dinner. Baba believed that there was strong magic in that branch.

"How do we use the branch?" Nom asks.

Zithembe finds a clay pot filled with plants and branches and starts to look through them carefully. He says, "We're going to use it to carry our spirits into the dreamworld."

"But we aren't dead! How can it

carry our spirits if we are still alive?"

"That's what we need the next thing for," Zithembe tells her. "It's a flower – the *gidla* flower. It's small, with very tiny petals. They are blue, white and gold."

Nom rolls her eyes and says, "No flowers are gold-coloured, Zithembe."

"This flower is. It's very special. The leaves of the flower are dark green with one orange stripe on the back. Let's split up: we need to find the *gidla* flower and the branches."

A glass cabinet behind Nom is filled with many different kinds of flowers. It is the most beautiful thing in this shop of horrors. Nom opens it and starts to look for the blue, white and gold flower.

After a few minutes she sees a packet of what must be the *gidla* flowers, and reaches out her hand – but as she does so she touches the petal of a bright purple flower, and the flower snaps shut over her finger. The flower is biting her and she screams and pulls her finger free. It comes out bleeding and Nom sticks it in her mouth. The taste of blood is salty and sweet.

Out of nowhere a man's voice booms behind her. "What are you doing in my shop, girl?"

Nom is so startled she jumps and turns around to see who is there. She quickly glances at Zithembe, and he seems startled too. In front of her stands an old man. He walks with a black cane and has brown teeth and a crooked back. Even bent over, he is still much taller than either Nom or Zithembe.

"Um …" Nom says, "I was just

looking around."

"For what?" the man asks.

Nom looks at Zithembe for some kind of support or explanation. He doesn't say anything.

"Ag, you kids! Always coming in here, trying to look at my things, wasting my time. Get out!" the man shouts. He shakes his stick at them, almost hitting Zithembe over the head.

Zithembe ducks and Nom grabs him by the shirt. They run to the door with the shop owner waving his cane and chasing close behind.

They hit the dirt and keep running. "Come back when you have money!" the old man shouts from his door.

"I found the branches, Nom – did you find the flower?" pants Zithembe, as they run, and Nom nods. It is much darker outside now. The shadows are long, and Nom imagines that she sees eyes in all of them.

When they are out of the neighbourhood, they slow down to a walk, and Zithembe tells Nom his plan: they need to break into the store and steal the supplies they need. Now that they have visited the shop in the daytime, they'll know exactly where to find what they are looking for under the cover of darkness.

"Why do we have to break in? I can get money," Nom says.

"Oh really? Everyone knows who your dad is and everyone knows I don't have any money. That means everyone's going to find out we were here. How are we going to explain why we were buying things from a shop like this? *Yho*, we can't take that kind of chance," Zithembe says.

Nom thinks it over as they walk. *Zithembe is probably right. We would not be able to answer questions about that shop or the dreamworld.* When they get home, it's properly dark. Nom tries to pull the gate open but it's already been locked. She bangs her fist on the gate and keeps banging until they hear someone unlocking the gate's heavy chain.

The gate opens just wide enough for Nom and Zithembe to go inside the yard. The taxi driver who opened the gate pulls it shut with a bang.

"*Sawubona*, Bra Solly," Zithembe says in greeting.

Solly nods at him but doesn't say a word. Zithembe and Nom see the bandage on his hand, and Nom asks what happened.

"That Mabegzo bit me on the way

back from the clinic," says Solly.

Zithembe and Nom look at each other. They can't believe a grown man has bit another grown man. This kind of thing only happens on the news, not in their home.

"Are you feeling OK, Solly?" Nom asks.

"Why do you ask?" Solly says. He turns his head, and in the light coming from the house Zithembe sees Solly's eyes flash yellow – just like Mabegzo's.

"We saw Mabegzo earlier. He was … acting strange," Nom says.

Solly turns around to make sure that no one is close by. When he turns back to Nom and Zithembe, he is smiling. His head snaps back in an unnatural way. Nom sucks in a small breath and takes a step backwards. Solly doesn't look like himself any more, breathing hard, with crazy eyes – he doesn't even look human. He looks like a monster

"My brothers and I, we come into this world. No more children. We will make sure that you are all gone. No one can stop us. You will all be gone," Solly says very slowly, very softly.

Solly lunges towards Zithembe and grabs him by both shoulders. Solly starts to lift Zithembe into the air. Zithembe tries to get loose, but Solly's bone-thin fingers dig deeper into the muscles of his shoulders. Zithembe cries out in pain.

Nom does not think; she just kicks Solly as hard as she can behind one of his knees. Solly's leg bends under him, he falls on one knee and he lets go of one of Zithembe's shoulders. Solly tries to grab Nom with his free hand, but she jumps out of the way and dives for the stones that line the grass in the front yard.

She grabs one stone in each hand and throws both of them at Solly. The first one hits Solly in the face, but he blocks the second one. As the stones hit, he lets go of Zithembe, who runs to Nom.

"*Yho*, Nom, you almost hit me with that stone!" Zithembe says.

Nom is scared but she can't help but roll her eyes. "Just run, Zee!"

They turn to run, but Solly grabs one of Nom's hands, dragging her towards him. Zithembe grabs a big stone from the ground and aims for Solly's head. Nom screams.

CHAPTER 6

The stone hits Solly in the ear just as Nom's dad, Bra Jabu, runs out of the house, barefoot and shirtless.

"Hey, *wena*!" shouts Jabu. "What are you doing with my girl?"

"Baba! Help me!" Nom shouts.

Solly is moaning and holding his ear. Jabu rushes towards him and throws a punch at his face. Solly falls and Jabu kicks him, but Solly grabs hold of Jabu's foot and bites down hard. Jabu cries out as Solly's teeth sink into his skin.

Nom and Zithembe watch in horror. Solly has bitten Jabu, which means that Jabu will soon become … whatever Solly is now – one of *them*. Solly lets go of Jabu's foot and rolls over onto his back. He laughs as the other drivers spill out into the yard from the garage, take hold of him and lift him to his feet.

One of the drivers asks Jabu, "What do you want us to do with him, boss?"

"Take him down to the police station!" Jabu barks back.

Solly keeps laughing as the drivers lead him to one of the taxis.

Nom's mom, Phumi, comes out of the house to see what's happening. She rushes to Jabu's side. "What happened?" she asks.

"Mama, Solly bit Baba," says Nom, blinking away tears.

"Bit him? Why?" asks Phumi.

"He's gone crazy," says Jabu.

"We have to get you some help. I'll call Dr Msibi to come to the house," says Phumi. She puts her arm around Jabu's waist to support him, and he limps back into the house with her.

Nom starts to follow them but Zithembe holds her back. "We have to leave tonight," he whispers. "There's no more time. We have to find out how to stop these monster things before anyone else gets hurt."

"We can meet at midnight," Nom says. "I'll come knock on your window. Be ready." She turns and goes into the house.

Zithembe walks around the house to the back rooms, where his aunt

Zinhle is making supper. They sit down to eat their pap and amasi. Zinhle asks him about school and homework, but he is too distracted to make conversation. He decides to leave the table early, telling his aunt that he feels sick.

A few hours later, Zithembe is lying in his bed, fully dressed and wide awake. He can hear his aunt snoring in the next room. He starts thinking about his parents and wishing that he had them around now. With all these scary things happening, he doesn't know if he is doing the right thing.

Before long he hears a knock at his small window. It must be Nom outside. He gets out of bed and picks up his takkies. In his socks, he creeps past his aunt's room and out of the back rooms.

"You ready, Zee?" Nom asks, zipping

up her school backpack and flinging it over one shoulder.

Zithembe finishes tying his shoes. "Let's go," he says.

They find their way to the shop much faster this time. When they get there, they find that the place is dark. The street light just outside the shop is broken. Nom and Zithembe find their way by the light of the full moon.

Zithembe gets to the door and takes out thick silver needles from his pocket. Nom checks to make sure that no one is around.

"There's no security here," she says.

"Not many people are stupid enough to steal from a shop like this," says Zithembe.

Of course, Nom thinks. *Most people are too scared of places like this to do something so crazy.*

The needles are thin enough to slide into the keyhole with no problem but also thick enough to move the lock. Zithembe fiddles with the needles for a few minutes until they hear a 'click' sound and the door opens.

"How did you learn to do that?" Nom says.

"What? Break into a house?" Zithembe asks. "Before I moved here, I was friends with some older boys who did a lot of stupid things. We broke into shops, they stole alcohol, we were wild."

Nom cannot imagine Zithembe ever doing anything like that. He thinks before he does everything; he's careful and he's responsible. Stealing from people and drinking do not sound like things Zithembe would do.

"So what happened?" Nom asks as

they tiptoe towards the *gidla* flowers.

"My friend got stabbed in a fight with some older boys in another gang. Gogo sent me here to live with Aunt Zinhle, and they made me promise I would stay out of trouble. I never wanted to get hurt or hurt anyone … The schools are better here too than in the village so it made sense."

Nom bumps her foot on one of the shelves "Ow! I just hit my big toe on something," she cries out. "I can't see a thing in here. We need some light."

Zithembe wants to stop her, but Nom is too fast. She removes her cellphone from her jacket pocket and turns on its flashlight. Light fills the small space.

Once again Zithembe shakes his head at his impulsive friend. But the light makes it much easier for him to find the clear plastic bags stuffed with *gidla* flowers lining the cabinets in the back.

"Now I just need to get the *umphafa* branches," he says.

In front of the pot with the branches sit two cats. They sit stiffly and stare as Nom and Zithembe without blinking. They're standing guard. One cat is black and the other is white. They look like they just woke up and they are not happy about it.

"I don't like cats," says Zithembe with a shaky voice. The cats hiss. The white one shows its sharp teeth.

"What? You're not scared of stealing but you're scared of cats?" Nom teases.

Zithembe starts to back away but the cats stalk towards him. Suddenly Nom starts barking like a dog. Zithembe looks at her like she is crazy, but the cats stop hissing. Their fur stands up on their backs. Nom barks louder and waves her arms around in all directions. Finally she rushes towards them, barking and shaking her arms and legs. The cats turn and run.

Nom laughs and Zithembe can't help but laugh too.

"You are crazy," he says, gently picking up the branches that they need, and wrapping them in newspaper before shoving them into Nom's backpack.

"I know," Nom says. "Come on, let's get out of here."

They run most of the way home, but they slow down when they hear singing just off the main road. Zithembe knows that the voices are coming from an empty plot full of nothing but rubbish, but Nom wants to take a look anyway.

"It is probably just a church group, Nom. We should get home," he says.

Nom ignores him and starts to jog towards the empty plot before Zithembe can stop her.

Zithembe follows her reluctantly. They hide behind a big, smelly dumpster and take a peak around the side of it. In the moonlight they can see a big pile of junk just a few feet away. On top of the heap, three people are dancing around and singing. Each of them wears newspapers instead of clothes. When they stop dancing, Zithembe pulls Nom back behind the dumpster. They crouch low and try not to make a sound. Suddenly they hear someone say, "I think I smell a person." The voice is Mabegzo's.

CHAPTER 7

Mabegzo says again, "I think I smell a person."

Nom and Zithembe stay quiet, hoping they won't be found.

One of the other monsters sniffs loudly and says, "Ag man, you are just imagining things. Everything here smells like people, but there's no people here." Nom and Zithembe recognise Solly's voice.

"It's all this junk," replies Mabegzo. "I can't smell properly with all this rubbish around."

Nom blindly claws around her and finds a banana peel on the ground. She rubs the peel on her neck and hands, trying to disguise her human smell. There's some mud on the ground too so she rubs that on her face. Zithembe realises what she is doing and does the same.

The three monsters start to sing and dance again. Nom sneaks a quick look at them: all their eyes glow bright green in the dark. There is no brown part left in their eyes – it's like there is nothing left of Mabegzo and Solly. The monsters inside them seem to wear their bodies as if they are clothes.

"We'll turn them into one of us, every last one!" they sing together.

"We'll send the children far away!"

"They'll never catch us!"

They all laugh, but they sound more like animals than people.

"They'll never stop us!"

The third monster speaks for the first time. "The time is now, brothers," he says. "We must turn everyone in my house into one of us." The voice is Bra Jabu's.

Nom puts her hand over her mouth, afraid that she will call out. Her father really has become one of the monsters.

"Tonight I will bite the mother," Jabu says. "You two get the other drivers. Don't forget Ma Zinhle. Then tomorrow, we get rid of the child, Nomthandazo, and also the other one, Zithembe. They both talk too much. When they are out of the way, we can find one of the Shadow Chaser knives. I can feel one of them is close by. I can feel its power but I don't know where it is. Once we have one of those knives, we can open up the doorway to the dreamworld and let our brothers and sisters into this world forever."

The three monsters hug and dance

and then move away together, in the direction of Nom's house. Zithembe and Nom stay hidden behind the dumpster until they can't hear the monsters any more.

They walk back to the house in silence, Zithembe carrying the backpack. Both of them are thinking about what they have just seen and heard. Nom notices a disgusting smell as they walk and wonders what it is. She sniffs around and then realises that what she is smelling is herself. She knows that she is still too scared to wash so she'll just have to get used to the smell.

"We can't let things go on like this," she tells Zithembe as they quietly open the front gate to the house. "We need to go to the dreamworld tonight, before it's too late."

Zithembe agrees. "We can make the *gidla* tea now. We've got the *umphafa* branches, and you need to make sure your knife is there – we'll need it later. We'll drink the tea and go into the dreamworld. There has to be a way to stop the monsters. I know the answer is in the dreamworld – I can feel it. I don't know how, but once we are there, we'll find out how to chase them away. There have to be some clues about what they are afraid of and what has power over them."

"And about how to save Baba," Nom says quietly.

Zithembe puts his hand on her shoulder and says, "Bra Jabu is tough, Nom. He will be OK."

Nom tries her best to believe him. She says, "We need to get the monsters out of Solly and Mabegzo too. Just like you said – we need to chase them out of our world and back to the dreamworld."

They creep quietly into the kitchen, and Nom puts the kettle on. Once the water is boiled, she carries two mugs of hot water to the table and sits opposite Zithembe. He puts the flowers into the mugs and stirs them into the water. The flowers dissolve in seconds.

"You have to go to bed with the knife under your pillow," Zithembe says, handing her a mug.

Then he gives her an *umphafa* branch.

"Put a branch on the floor next to you, and when you wake up, you won't be in the real world. You'll be at a doorway to the dreamworld. It's like a waiting place between the real world and the dreamworld. There will be magic there – enough magic to take you into dreamworld.

"I'll meet you in the kitchen at your house in the dream. We have to use your knife to open the door. I'm not sure if we cut through the door or use the knife as a key or force it open. We'll have to work that out when we get there."

Nom bites her lip and looks down. "It seems like there's a lot of things we don't know, Zee," she says.

Zithembe shrugs. "I don't know, Nom. I've only heard Mama's stories about this. But I don't think she would lie to me."

Nom notices a small label on the packet of *gidla* flowers. "What does that say?" she asks, pointing to the packet.

Zithembe reads aloud: "The flowers are like matches to dry wood. They will light the fire in me. I do not open my eyes. It is not with my eyes that I see. My ancestors see for me. I see in a dream."

Nom wraps her fingers around the hot mug. "Here we go," she says.

They both gulp their tea, and take their branch. Zithembe sneaks out of the house and Nom somehow stumbles to her room. She already feels like she is half-asleep. Nom lies down on her bed. *When I wake up, I'll be in the dreamworld,* she thinks. *My ancestors see for me, I see in a dream* … Her eyelids are too heavy to stay open. She must sleep now – the dreamworld is waiting.

CHAPTER 8

Nom thinks that she will fall into a
deep sleep, but as soon as she closes
her eyes, she finds herself wide awake.
She sits up in her bed, thinking, *The tea
didn't work.* She decides to get up and
get a glass of water. But as soon as she
puts one foot onto the floor, she knows
something isn't quite right.

The hard tiled floor is usually cold
in the night, but the surface under her

foot is soft and warm. Nom laughs and jumps out of bed. She bounces off the floor. When she lands and jumps up again, she springs up so high she hits her head on the ceiling. When her feet touch back down on the floor, she tries again.

This time she takes a very small jump and she finds herself floating in the air. Nom floats around her room, turning her body around and around, making herself dizzy. Now she can't stop laughing. This must be the waiting place, the in-between place that Zee talked about. The doorway to the dreamworld is nearby.

Nom is amazed that she is able to fly and float around in the dreamworld. It feels so free and magical that she doesn't want to just walk like she usually does. Then she remembers what the plan is. She can't play games now. Nom allows herself to float back down to the floor.

Zee and I both took the umphafa branches and drank the gidla flower tea, she recalls. *We agreed that if we woke up in the dreamworld, we would both go back to the kitchen in my house. Once we are together again, we will find the door and then figure out what to do next.*

Nom reaches under her pillow for her knife. She feels the cold metal warm up at her touch. She pulls it out, and in this waiting place the knife glows a pale-blue colour. It looks like it is alive.

"Cool," Nom says quietly. She wants Zee to see this. She needs to find him.

Nom takes her knife, jumps up lightly and floats to her bedroom door. She pulls at the handle, but it's locked. She pushes the door, pulls it, hits it, scratches it with her knife. Nothing works. A pale-blue light shines out of the keyhole, but when she tries to peer through to see what's on the other side, she's blinded by the unnatural blue light. *Zee will know what to do*, she thinks. He is the one with the plans; she's the one who brings the action.

She's about to go back to bed when she looks down at the knife and then at the keyhole. The blue glow of her knife matches the light coming in from the other side of the closed door. Nom pushes the knife blade into the keyhole. To her surprise it fits perfectly – just like a key. She turns the knife and hears a click. She tries the door handle. The door opens.

Nom expects to see the passage in her house beyond the open door. She expects to see Zee waiting for her on the other side, so that they can go into the dreamworld together. Instead, the door opens onto a beautiful garden.

Nom turns back to make sure she's still in her room, but now her room isn't there any more either. It has disappeared. She turns back to the door and that has disappeared too. Now she is just floating in the air, above a huge garden. The garden is filled with flowers of all sizes and colours. All she can see are rows and rows of blooms.

She is in the dreamworld. But she is alone.

"Hello?" Nom calls out. "Zee? Zithembe, are you here?"

There is no reply. It feels like she is the only person in the dreamworld.

Nom wishes that she was not alone, and as she thinks it, she hears someone speaking behind her.

"Nomthandazo?" says a woman's voice.

Nom floats back down onto the soft soil. She tries not to stand on any of the flowers, but then she remembers that she's not in a real garden. Everything around her exists only in the dreamworld.

Nom turns around to see a woman dressed like a farmer in ugly brown overalls. The woman takes off her hat and wipes sweat off her forehead with her arms. Her skin is very dark and she has no hair under her hat.

"How do you know my name?" asks Nom.

The woman shakes her head and says, "Why are you here?"

Nom folds her arms. "Answer my question first, please. How do you know my name?"

Nom starts to hear strange, animal sounds not too far away from them. There is the sound of a very big bird crying out. Then she hears what sounds like a family of monkeys all screeching and screaming at each other. Finally there are the sounds of girls laughing and laughing. Nom has heard the bullies at her school laugh like that before. Those girls are always happiest when they are doing something bad.

The woman turns her head towards the sounds and frowns. "It isn't safe for you out here in the garden," she says. "Any one of the monsters in the Army could find us. You have to think of a house, a house that is hidden. Only we will be able to see that house. We'll be able to hide there."

Nom doesn't move and she forces

herself not to think of anything. "Why do I need to think of that?" she asks.

The woman sighs just like Zithembe would if he was here. She says, "In the dreamworld, everything you *think* is what will happen. If you think that you are hungry, food will suddenly appear. If you think that you are cold, a blanket will be right there. You have to think of a house for us to hide in!"

"I'm not doing or thinking anything until you tell me who you are," says Nom.

"My name is Itumeleng," the woman says. "I am one of the *Bhekizizwe*, the Shadow Chasers, and I am also Zithembe's mother."

CHAPTER 9

"What?" Nom asks.

"Nomthandazo, we don't have
time for this now. Think of a house –
quickly!" Itumeleng says.

Nom does what Itumeleng says. She
closes her eyes and takes a deep breath.
Nom tries to think of the kind of house
she's seen on TV. A house surrounded
by trees and a high brick wall to protect
it. A house made of wood with a big

bedroom for her and one for Zithembe. One that smells like Gogo's cooking all the time and where she can have chocolate anytime she wants.

"You did it!" says Itumeleng.

Nom opens her eyes to see that the garden has vanished. In its place the house she was just thinking of has appeared.

"Wow," Nom says, staring in amazement at the house.

Itumeleng pushes her from behind in the direction of the front door. "We have to hurry."

"OK, OK," says Nom. "I'm going!"

Itumeleng opens the front door and steps aside so Nom can enter. The smell of Gogo's cooking is everywhere. Nom heads straight for the pile of chocolate on the table in the TV room.

While she is unwrapping her first

chocolate, they hear the sound of something big landing on the roof. The whole house seems to shake.

"What was that?" Nom asks.

"You have your Shadow Chaser's knife, don't you? That's the only way you can enter the dreamworld. It's also the only way to make wishes in the dreamworld," Itumeleng replies. "But the monster that trapped me here took away my knife: my wishes don't come true any more.

"The thing is, the dreamworld can also make your nightmares come true. That's what is happening now. The Army knows you are here, they can feel your magic. So they sent some of your nightmares here to find you."

Nom is on the verge of remembering all the bad dreams she's ever had, but she immediately stops herself. In this world, whatever she thinks of can actually happen. She has to be careful about where she lets her mind go.

Nom puts down her chocolate and takes a deep breath. "What did you say about a monster trapping you here? And what is this Army you were talking about?"

"You have a lot of questions, *bathong*," Itumeleng says, smiling. It's the first time that Nom has seen her smile. She realises that Zithembe has his mother's smile.

Nom doesn't say anything but waits to hear Itumeleng speak. What Zithembe's mother knows is important, and Nom feels they may not have very much time to talk. She can hear what she thinks are monkeys climbing the trees around the house. Nom hates monkeys.

"I am a Shadow Chaser," Itumeleng says, "which means that I am part of a special group of people who are meant to protect people in the real world from the monsters in the dreamworld. Your aunt was a Shadow Chaser, you are a Shadow Chaser and so is Zithembe."

"I don't even know what a Shadow Chaser *is*."

"You will learn. You must learn. The Army of Shadows is getting stronger. It is an army of monsters. We call them the Army of Shadows because they live in the dark of the dreamworld; they are the worst monsters in this place.

"The Army wants to destroy all joy in the world. The Army monsters are all like the monsters you are fighting at home – the Army wants to get rid of all children and take over. When they do, all nightmares will come true. No one will be safe."

"But we're just twelve-year-olds – what can we do?"

"You have magic, you are brave, you can do anything. And you and Zithembe have the knives."

Those must be the Shadow Chaser knives Nom heard the monsters talking about. Is her knife one of those? If she's a Shadow Chaser, it must be. But Zee doesn't have a knife. Nom shakes her head and says, "There's only one knife, the one that my aunt left for me. Zee doesn't have a knife."

Itumeleng's eyes fill with tears. "But what about Zithembe's knife?" she asks. "I left my brother's knife for Zithembe. I hid it in the village; I thought my mother would tell him where to look for it after I disappeared … Where is his knife?"

"I don't know. I don't think Zee knows either. He never said anything about having a knife to me," Nom says.

Itumeleng still looks like she may cry. She hugs her arms around herself, closes her eyes and takes two deep breaths. Nom can't imagine what it must be like to be trapped here, to be away from her son, to not be able to go home, and to live hunted by this shadow army of monsters.

Itumeleng opens her eyes. "Did you know that your father and Zee's parents were from the same village, emaKhosini?" she asks.

Nom shrugs and says, "I didn't know that … from emaKhosini, the Place of Kings? Daddy tells me stories about when he was growing up there."

Itumeleng smiles and explains, "In the stories about how the village started hundreds of years ago, before the wars of men and before our country even had a name, four families lived in emaKhosini village.

"They were warriors and they had six magical knives between them. Zee's father came from the Nkala family, you and your late aunt from the Masina family and I was from the Batlokoa family. There was a fourth family too, the Belebeleni family.

"The families used the knifes to protect people from the Army of Shadows. Their knives were not like other knives – they were not for violence or pain. These were magical, remember? They gave them many powers …

"So you see, Nom, you have to find Zee's knife. Zee can't come into this world without it. You can't defeat the

Army of Shadows without it. If his knife
is also missing, that means there are
at least two Shadow Chasers' lives in
danger: his and mine. Promise me that
you will find it."

"I promise," says Nom.

They listen to the sounds of the
mean girls laughing outside. The
laughter reminds her of those bullies,
the Trouble Gurlz.

"Where is your knife?" Nom asks
Itumeleng.

Itumeleng shakes her head and says,
"I don't know. When the monsters took
me, they took my knife too. I can't
get back to the real world without my
knife. Each knife only works for its
Shadow Chaser.

"They are our keys in and out of
the dreamworld, but they can work for
the Army of Shadows too. One of them

stole my knife just after they caught me and trapped me here.

"No one has seen it since that night and I've been stuck here ever since. I have tried to think of it, to dream it back to me many times but magical things are never easy …"

"Then we will find your knife too. We'll help you escape this place and come home," Nom says. Nom thinks about Zee, about how happy he will be to know for sure that his mother is really alive. She loves him, she wants to come home and she is alive.

Itumeleng smiles. Nom smiles back, but the warm feelings of friendship and trust disappear quickly when she remembers why she came here to begin with.

"I fought with your aunt, you know. She was a very brave woman. Just like you," Itumeleng explains.

Nom says quietly, "I don't feel very brave, Ma Itumeleng. There are monsters in my house. I heard what they said. They are looking for a Shadow Chaser's knife – my knife."

Itumeleng nods. "Just like I told you – our knives are magic. They want to use the knife to cut open a hole to the dreamworld and let all the monsters loose on our world. We have to stop them before they find the knife, before it's too late."

"But now they have my Baba. He's turned into one of them. How can I save him?"

"What kind of monsters are they?" Itumeleng asks.

"We don't know … They have shining green eyes. They were howling and dancing together too," Nom says.

Itumeleng takes a minute to think. "They sound like Eats."

"What are 'Eats'?" asks Nom.

"They are soldiers in the Army of Shadows. They are called Eats because they eat children."

Nom feels her body go cold with fear. She closes her eyes and takes a deep breath. The fear is fading when she asks, "How do we get rid of them?"

Itumeleng folds her arms and frowns. "You can use your knife to kill them, but you would kill the people they are living inside too," she says.

"No!" Nom shouts.

"There is another way ... the *gidla* tea! You could make them drink the *gidla* tea without their knowing it. It will force them out of the bodies they stole and back into the dreamworld. They will be trapped here like me."

Nom says, "You mean, make the tea, and then trick them into drinking it? Got it."

"Then you are ready," Itumeleng says. She stretches her hand out and touches Nom's cheek. "Time to go, sweetie."

"How do I get back to the real world?" Nom asks.

"Just close your eyes, lie down and think of home. Think of being awake and safe in your bed, and when you wake up, that is where you will be. The knife is your guide: as long as you have it, you will always be able to find your way home."

"What about you? Can't you come with me?"

Itumeleng shakes her head. "You will save me, Nomthandazo. That is part of your destiny. You are *Bhekizizwe,* a Shadow Chaser, just like me, just like Zithembe. It is your job to fight the Army of Shadows. You and Zithembe will free me from this prison, but not tonight. You must first go home and save your father."

"What about you?" Nom asks. The noises from outside are getting louder. Those things outside are trying to break the door down.

Itumeleng flashes her best smile and takes a small leather bag out of her back pocket. She undoes the knot tying the bag closed and tips a tiny bit of shiny, blue powder in the bag out into her own palm. The powder catches the light and there is a flash of white and silver as Itumeleng holds out her hand for Nom to see.

"What is it?" Nom asks, not able to stop staring at Itumeleng's powder.

"It's magic, of course," Itumeleng says. "It's a powder I use to turn myself invisible. I just throw some of it above my head and as it falls on me, it makes me invisible so that no one and no monster can see me. Some of them can still smell me, of course, but that's why I learned to run fast and hide too."

"Can I take some back with me? Will it work outside of the dreamworld?"

"Of course. You only need a small amount for it to work," agrees Itumeleng. Nom holds out her hand and Itumeleng sprinkles a tiny bit of blue powder into her hand.

Itumeleng hugs Nom tightly, "Use the magic powder carefully. Tell Zee that I love him and I'll see him soon. Find our knives."

Nom closes her eyes, holds tight onto her knife with her one hand and clutches her powder in the other. She thinks of home just as the front door explodes. Everything goes dark.

CHAPTER 10

Nom sits up in her bed bathed in sweat. She stinks and she's still wearing last night's clothes. She rubs her eyes and runs over all the information she now knows: *It's Saturday morning, so no school. Monsters exist. The Army of Shadow must be defeated.* She's still holding her knife in one hand and her powder in the other.

Nom hears someone coming to her

room. She stuffs the powder in one pocket and the knife under her pillow.

Her mother bursts through the door. Suddenly Nom is being pulled out of bed by one arm. She looks up to see her mother clenching her arm tightly.

"Mama!" she cries out in pain.

Phumi looks down at Nom and smiles. Her eyes flash that scary green colour.

"I'm not your mommy, little girl," the monster in her mom's body says. Nom's heart beats hard and she can feel the blood rushing fast through her body. Not her mother too!

The monster pulls Nom to the kitchen, where Solly has Zithembe by the shirt. Mabegzo and Jabu sit at the table, drinking hot tea with biscuits.

"What now, boss?" Solly asks Jabu.

"For now, we lock them up and

make sure that everyone in the house is like us. After that, we're going to send these two brats to the dreamworld forever!"

Nom and Zithembe are thrown into the cupboard where Ma Zinhle keeps the cleaning stuff. It is barely big enough for them both to stand inside with the mops and brooms. The door is locked. It's totally black inside. They wait for their eyes to adjust while listening to the sound of all the monsters leaving the kitchen. Only then do they speak.

Nom is frightened but now is the time to be brave. They have to be calm and think. She has to save her parents from the monsters who are living inside them! She takes a deep breath and tries to make a joke. "Well, that was a rude way to be woken up," she whispers.

"And now we're stuck in here."

"Not for long," whispers Zithembe. He pulls out two small pins from his back pocket. "I can break us out of here from the inside, but we need a plan once we're out."

Nom thinks, trying to remember what Zithembe's mom said the night before. *Make the tea, make sure that the monsters drink it.* But before they do that, she has to tell Zithembe what happened last night.

"I saw your mom, Zee. She was in the dreamworld," Nom blurts out. She explains everything: how she could fly in the dreamworld, the monsters that live there, the house she made with her mind, how Itumeleng had told her about the Shadow Chasers and the Army of Shadows, and that the monsters are looking for her knife.

"She said that you have a knife like mine because we are both Shadow Chasers," Nom says when she finishes her story.

"Then we have to find it … *Yho*, I can't believe Mama is alive." Zithembe puts his face in his hands.

"She's alive, but trapped. We have to find her knife too. The knife is her key out of the dreamworld."

"We have to get her out," Zithembe says in a quiet but determined voice. He wants to cry from joy that his mother is all right, from sadness that she is trapped somewhere he cannot go and from fear that the Army may keep him from his mother forever.

Nom does not know what else to do so she rubs Zithembe's back. "We will," she says. "We'll find your knives and get her out. But first, we need to get rid of these monsters in our house."

He looks up and says, "I know. What do we do?"

"We need to pour the rest of the *gidla* flowers into their coffee. Your mom said that it will send them back into the dreamworld, where they came from," Nom explains.

"But how do we do that? They won't just let you walk right up to the coffee?" Zithembe asks.

"They won't even know I'm there," Nom explains, digging in her pocket for the pinch of invisibility powder that Itumeleng gave her. Nom raises her hand above her head and carefully sprinkles the powder on her head, making sure not to drop or waste any.

Zithembe watches as Nom starts to disappear. His mouth hangs open, his eyes go wide – Zithembe is sure he doesn't fully even understand what they are seeing. First her head becomes invisible, then her shoulders and soon he can't see anything of her.

"Nom?" Zithembe asks, uncertain about whether she is even still there.

Nom shoves him playfully, "Right here, Zee," she whispers, giggling.

"What … what was that? What did you just do? *How* did you just do that?" Zithembe stammers.

"Your mom gave me a magic powder. She uses it in the dreamworld to escape from the Army of Shadows when they trap her somewhere – like they were trying to do in the house I imagined for us to hide in."

"Wow," is all Zithembe can say.

"OK, I'm ready to do my part. Can you get me out of here?" Nom asks.

Zithembe immediately starts to work

on the lock. It takes much longer for him to pick this lock than the one at the shop. At last they hear the click of the lock sliding open.

"Good job, Zee!" whispers Nom. "You watch the door. I'll poison their water with the flowers. Warn me if you see any of them coming – whistle or something, OK?"

Nom pushes the door of the cupboard open just a little bit. A small strip of sunlight sneaks through the crack. There's no one in the kitchen, so Nom steps out of the cupboard and fetches the *gidla* flowers from her room. Back in the kitchen, she quickly empties the plastic bag of flowers into the kettle. They dissolve in seconds.

Nom hears Zithembe whistle behind her. She spins around to see the Eats coming into the kitchen – about to walk right in to her. Jabu, Phumi and Solly rush towards her but before she can even react, Zithembe jumps out of the cupboard. They all turn in his direction at the flash of movement so Nom sneaks towards the safety of one of the kitchen walls.

Zithembe tries to get to the kitchen's back door, but Zinhle grabs his arm before he gets there. Nom presses herself as flat as possible against the wall and tries not to breathe.

"I'm tired of you two," says Jabu. "And I'm hungry. I think we need to get rid of you for good. Does anyone want some child curry?"

"Where is the girl?" Phumi asks, sniffing the air. The others do the same but they can't smell her. Nom doesn't smell like a girl right now – she didn't have a chance to bath so she still smells like the rubbish from last night.

"Mabegzo!" Jabu barks, "Go! Find her now!"

Mabegzo leaves the house in search of Nom while Phumi and Solly tie Zithembe to the leg of the kitchen table.

"Let me go! Let me go!" Zithembe shouts. He kicks and struggles to get free but he's tied up tight and he's not going anywhere.

Ma Zinhle takes out spices from the cupboard while Solly collects some vegetables. They all go out the back door to the courtyard, where they do the outside cooking. A huge black cooking pot sits there waiting. Jabu starts to build a fire around the pot while Solly fills it with water.

Then Solly unties Zithembe from the kitchen table and carries him outside.

Zithembe is still kicking and fighting
to get free when Solly lifts and puts
him into the cooking pot. Ma Zinhle
sprinkles all the spices she collected
into the water around him and over his
heads.

The water hasn't started to heat up yet, but the fire is starting to get going. Meanwhile all the monsters are laughing and joking with each other. It looks like it's going to be breakfast time very soon. And Zithembe is on the menu.

CHAPTER 11

Jabu goes inside the house for a few minutes while the others keep an eye on Zithembe in the pot. Nom is scared and can hear Zithembe shouting from outside but her heart has started to beat slower now that she knows for sure that the Eats can't see or smell her.

Just as they had planned, Jabu pours the poisoned coffee into four mugs and returns to the fire outside with steaming mugs of coffee for all the other Eats. They drink to their victory.

The water must be starting to heat up. Nom has to do something to save Zithembe – who knows how long the poison will take to work. Suddenly Nom gets an idea. She rushes outside quietly, tiptoes around Phumi and Solly, and reaches the pot that Zithemebe is stuck in.

Nom leans all her weight onto the handle of the pot. It starts to tip slightly. Feeling the pot start to fall, Zithembe shifts his body weight in the same direction as Nom is pushing. The pot tips over completely. The water spills everywhere, killing the fire, and Zithembe lands on the ground totally wet. The monsters all drop their mugs.

The monsters stare at Zithembe who is coughing and wriggling on the ground but Nom starts to pick up the wood from the fire and throw it at them.

"It's the girl!" Jabu shouts, "She is invisible!"

Nom rushes back into the kitchen, flings open the cupboard closest to the door and starts throwing mugs, plates, glasses – anything she can find really – out the door, towards the monsters in the outdoor cooking area.

The Eats forget about Zithembe and march quickly into the kitchen. Nom ducks and dives to avoid Zinhle but Phumi catches Nom by the shoulder, digging her nails into Nom's skin.

Nom cries out in pain so that all the Eats know exactly where she is now and the sound of her shouting sends a new fear rushing through Zithembe. He struggles to sit up but still can't get loose.

"Got you, little girl. Thought you were clever, hey? Thought you could escape us, huh?" Solly and Jabu laugh as they stalk closer to Nom. Then – as suddenly as they found Nom – the monsters suddenly come to an abrupt halt, frozen in place. They can move their eyes, but nothing else. They stand like statues – then they all fall down.

Nom falls to the ground with Phumi. At first she is still in shock about what just happened but the sound of Zithembe calling her brings her back to her senses.

She stumbles up and out. As she goes she notices that she is no longer invisible. Zithembe is sitting on the ground, wet and still tied up.

"I can't get free. You need to cut these ropes," Zithembe says.

Nom quickly goes back into the

kitchen, avoiding the bodies on the floor as best as she can, and finds the sharp knife her mother tells her never to touch.

She is back outside in less than a minute and tries to hack away at the rope around Zithembe. Nothing happens. The knife is doing nothing to the ropes.

"I don't understand ..." Nom says, shaking her head. "This is the sharpest knife in the house."

"Nom, the rope is probably magic somehow. We need magic to defeat magic."

"Of course! My knife!" Nom realises out loud. "We can use my knife to cut us free."

As soon as she has said the words out loud, Nom's knife flies out of the house and into her hand gracefully.

Shocked, Nom and Zithembe just look from the knife to each other and back to the knife for a few seconds.

"How did you *do* that?" asks Zithembe.

"My knife ... it just flew into my hand. I just thought about it – I didn't do anything! It just did it by itself, Zee!" says Nom.

Zithembe shakes his head, not sure whether he really believes that knives can fly. After everything he's seen in the last two days, though, he shouldn't even be surprised.

The rope falls away easily from Zithembe. With her knife in hand, Nom helps Zithembe to his feet and they walk back into the house.

"Are they ... OK?" Nom asks, seeing the bodies lying where she left them. She doesn't want to think the worst, but her mom and dad aren't moving.

Zithembe kneels down between Jabu and Phumi and puts his hand under Jabu's nose. He feels his warm breath go in and out.

"They're just sleeping," says Zithembe, turning back to Nom.

Just then Mabegzo walks into the house. He looks at Solly, Jabu, Phumi and Zinhle sleeping on the floor. He looks at the tipped-over pot. He looks at Zithembe and Nom. He takes two steps forward, and Nom suddenly steps in front of Zithembe to protect him. She holds up her knife in front of her to keep Mabegzo away. Only now does she see that her knife is glowing a hot-red colour.

Mabegzo's eyes go wide and he says, "*You* two are Shadow Chasers? All this time we had the knife right here, so

close, and we didn't even know it …
You may think you're clever, but the
Army of Shadows will not be defeated
so easily. You may have won today, but
I will see you Shadow Chasers again
soon. Next time, I'll be ready for you."

Mabegzo freezes and his eyes shine
green one last time. Green slime comes
out of his nose and runs down over his
mouth and neck. His eyes turn back to
their normal colour and Mabegzo falls
to the ground, just as suddenly as the
others. He is fast asleep.

Nom and Zithembe collapse into the
chairs at the kitchen table. It's finally
over.

"Whoa – this is crazy. Do you think
the monsters are really gone?" Nom
asks Zithembe.

"I think they are only gone for
now. You heard Mabegzo. We may be

Shadow Chasers, but we don't even really know what that means. And the Army of Shadows will be back," says Zithembe. "We should get some sleep too. We may have some explaining to do when everyone wakes up."

"Can we just leave them here?" Nom asks.

Zithembe laughs. "I don't think they're going to wake up anytime soon. We have to leave them."

Zithembe walks with Nom to her bedroom. She crawls into her bed and he sits on the floor next to the *umphafa* branch. Nom is careful not to put the knife under her pillow, just in case it accidentally sends her into the dreamworld. Instead, she puts it safely under her bed.

Neither of them has spoken for a few minutes when Nom asks, "Zee, what do you think is going to happen next? How are we going to fight a whole army of monsters? How are we going to find your knife? How are we going to find your mom's knife so that we can bring her back?"

When Zithembe doesn't reply, Nom looks down and sees that he is fast asleep right there on her bedroom floor. She sighs softly to herself, closes her eyes and falls asleep.

CHAPTER 12

When Nom wakes up, the sun is
setting. Zee is no longer sleeping in her
room. She hopes that he woke up and
sneaked back to his own room before
anyone saw him.

She puts the *umphafa* branch away
carefully, inside her cupboard. Who
knows when she will need it again?

Nom stumbles to the kitchen,
rubbing sleep out of her eyes. Phumi

and Ma Zinhle are busy cooking. Pots cover the stovetops. Jabu and Mabegzo are sitting at the table, eating chicken and pap with their hands.

"Nomthi!" her mother says. "Have you been sleeping all day?"

Before Nom can reply, Jabu says, "Ah, Phumi, leave her alone. We all woke up late today."

Nom gives her dad a big hug and asks, "How are you feeling, Baba? Are you ... OK?"

"Sure, Nomthi, I'm fine, my child. What would be wrong with me?"

"Oh nothing ... I was just asking," Nom says, sitting down with a small plate of food. "Mama, Ma Zinhle, how are you?"

"We're all fine, Nomthi. The only thing is that everybody in this house woke up very hungry and we've been cooking and eating all day! I don't know what got into us last night!" says Ma Zinhle.

Jabu stops eating and says, "You know, there was one thing – I had the strangest dream …"

"Really?" Nom asks. "What did you dream about?"

Her dad rubs the back of his neck and looks up at the ceiling, trying to remember. "I was dancing – and singing – in that empty veld with the rubbish down the street. And Solly and Mabegzo were there with me," he says.

"You, Solly and Mabegzo dancing and singing? *Hai*! That is something I would pay money to see!" says Ma Zinhle.

"We must have been drunk in your dream, Bra Jabu. That's the only explanation!" says Mabegzo.

Everyone laughs.

Zithembe walks into the kitchen and Nom runs up to hug him. "Zee! Come sit with us," she says excitedly, pulling him to the table. "My dad is telling a story about a crazy dream he had last night."

Zithembe sits next to Nom at the table and Ma Zinhle passes him a plate.

Bra Jabu looks at Nom and then at Zithembe and back at Nom. "Since when were you two such big buddies, huh?" her dad asks, between mouthfuls of food.

Nom laughs and says, "Oh Baba, you wouldn't believe us even if we did tell you!"

Zithembe just shakes his head while Nom laughs and the grown-ups just look at each other, not understanding the joke.

Nom can't stop thinking about everything that has happened: defeating the Eats, finding the dreamworld, meeting Zee's mom, being told that she's a Shadow Chaser. She looks over at Zithembe. He's frowning. She imagines that he's thinking what she's thinking: the fight has just begun.

"We'll find your knife, Zee. And then together we'll find Itumeleng's knife, to bring her back. We'll stop the Army of Shadows for good. I promise," Nom says quietly.

Zithembe gives her a grateful smile. Together, they may just have a chance.

THE END

Can't wait to get started on Book 2 of *Shadow Chasers*? Read on ...

CHAPTER 1

Nom turns her head just in time to see the big stick swinging towards her head. She ducks down fast and folds herself flat in the dust. Above her, Nom hears the stick swoosh through the air and she rolls away from the sound.

Pushing herself out of the dirt in 10 seconds flat, she is alert and ready for the next attack. Her own stick is heavy in her hand as she swings it upwards at her dad's head. Bra Jabu, Nom's father, side-steps and avoids her stick with ease. In the same movement, Jabu lifts him stick above his head and brings it down to tap Nom's shoulder lightly.

Their referee, Zithembe – Nom's best friend, maybe her only friend – claps and laughs. "Two points to Bra Jabu!"

he announces.

"It's not fair!" Nom says, "You're bigger than me, Baba."

"Not every fight is fair, Nomthi. And you're faster than I am," her father says, "I'm not teaching you stick fighting so that you can run around beating people up. You have to learn patience, how to watch your opponent and understand what they are thinking and what they'll do next. It doesn't matter if they are bigger – you have to be smarter."

"But I can still beat people up if I have to, right Baba?" Nom says with a naughty smile.

Now Jabu laughs, "You remind me of when I was your age, growing up in emaKhosini – I was just as silly as you are."

"emaKhosini?" asks Zithembe.

Jabu nods and says, "The Place of

Kings. That's the village your father and I grew up in. We used to practice just like this on the beach … Actually, your aunt and Zithembe's mother, Itumeleng, used to practice with us. They won every time we played with them – it was embarrassing but sometimes girls are just better fighters than us boys!" he adds with a wink to Zithembe.

Nom and Zithembe's eyes meet. They are both serious now, thinking the same thing. Nom's aunt and Zithembe's mother were both Shadow Chasers – just like Nom and Zithembe are now. And Itumeleng is trapped in the dreamworld, hunted by a shadow army of monsters that she can't escape without Nom and Zithembe's help.

In the weeks since they found out about the Army of Shadows, the secrets of their families and their magical knives, Nom and Zithembe have thought about nothing else. They have talked day and night about how to find the knives that belong to Zithembe and Itumeleng, and how to break Itumeleng out of the dreamworld. They haven't had any idea of where to even start looking for Zithembe's knife – until now. emaKhosini, the Place of Kings, is where all this began. Hundreds of years ago, four warrior families lived in the village. It was the home of the first Shadow Chasers. Maybe it also holds the clue they've been looking for? Maybe it holds a way to rescue Itumeleng?

Nom says exactly what she's thinking, "We should go to emaKhosini! Zee and I."